Foreword

There is a little corner of England called Copford Green, in Essex. In a corner of that corner lies a church called Copford Church. The church is long on history, having been built by the Normans in the 12th century. It is big on surprises too, having the oldest recorded wall paintings of any parish church in Britain.

Like many churches in Britain, Copford St Michael & All Angels is long on name but rather short on funds. It has delicate wall paintings that need to be preserved. It has an ash-shingled spire that falls prey to the beaks of the local woodpeckers.

The Mice in the Churchyard is not the story of Copford Church. It is the story of a local author working with the Friends of Copford Church to help secure its future for a further 900 years. I have written this book for love, not money. I have waived my author fees, and any royalties due to me will be donated to the church fund.

All of the cats mentioned in this story are (or have been) whiskered residents of the parish. My thanks to every parishioner who has forwarded photographs of their cats to me. My apologies to any cat who, for one reason or another, may have been overlooked. All of the two-legged characters in this story are long gone, but forever respected residents of the graveyard. Their silent consent is much appreciated too.

The Mice in the Churchyard has been a challenge to write but a mountainous task to illustrate. My towering thanks go to Sally Anne Lambert who has proved more than equal to the task. A story like this is nothing without a publisher. Praise be to Bloomsbury, who has not only championed this rather unusual cause, but will endeavour to market and promote this story across the Atlantic and throughout the cat-loving world.

KES GRAY

To the village ~ *KG*

For Jonny and Katie, with love ~ *SAL*

Bloomsbury Publishing, London, New Delhi, New York and Sydney
First published in Great Britain in 2013 by Bloomsbury Publishing Plc
50 Bedford Square, London, WC1B 3DP

Text copyright © Kes Gray 2013
Illustrations copyright © Sally Anne Lambert 2013
The moral rights of the author and illustrator have been asserted

A CIP catalogue record of this book is available from the British Library

ISBN 978 1 4088 3856 3

Printed in China

3 5 7 9 10 8 6 4 2

All papers used by Bloomsbury Publishing are natural, recyclable products made
from wood grown in well-managed forests. The manufacturing processes
conform to the environmental regulations of the country of origin

www.bloomsbury.com

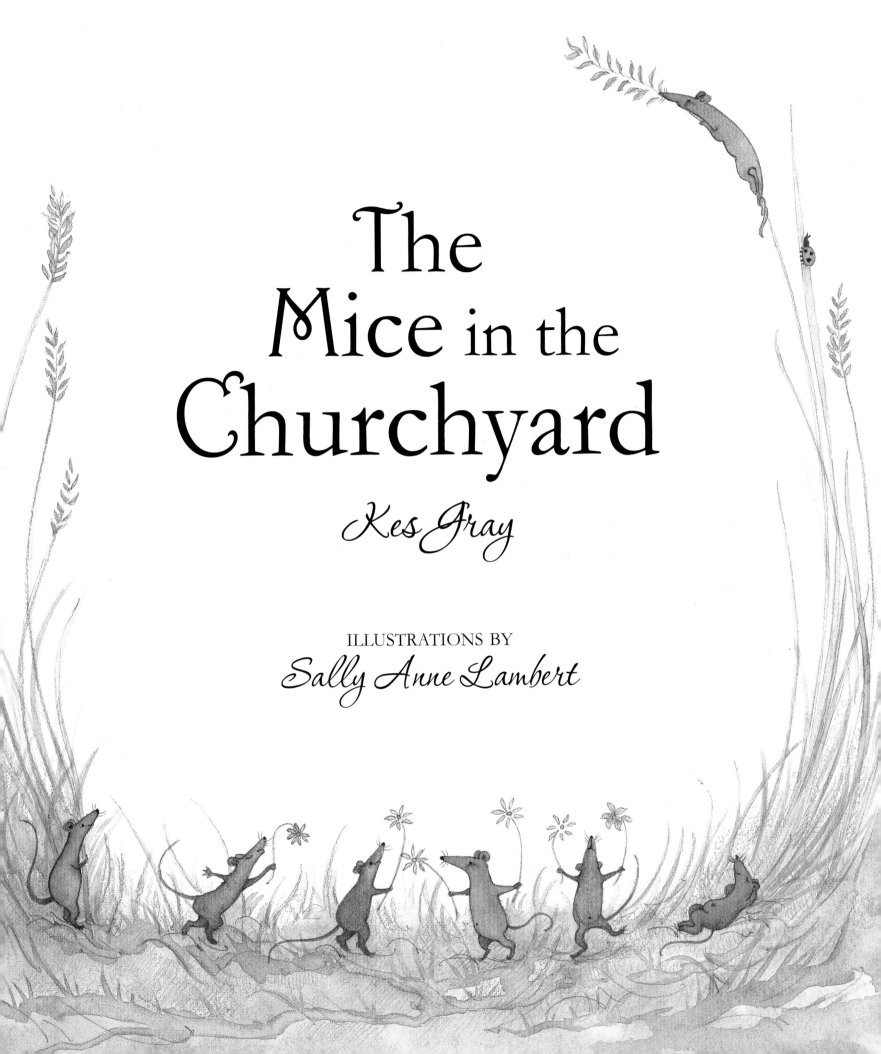

The
Mice in the
Churchyard

Kes Gray

ILLUSTRATIONS BY

Sally Anne Lambert

Ah the mice in the churchyard, they run free,
Dance in the daylight, bold as can be.
Flit through the grasses, play in the sun,
Wave at the neighbourhood cats just for fun.
"I hate them!" spat Felix. "They're so in our face!
It's time that the cats in this parish gave chase!"

That night the cats held a mouse-catching meeting,
Using tombstones for tables and headstones for seating.
Word travelled fast and attendance was strong,
Even Maggie the Short Hair padded along.
Hamish McTavish was first through the gate,
Kitty and Minnow had made it a date.
Miffy and Midnight, Daisy and Smartie,
Pink and both Jazzes had all joined the party.

Bonny and Clyde emerged from a spinney,

Mr Bowlegs dropped by with Dillon and Minnie.

There was Edge, there was Bono, Muffin and Fred,

There was Mickey and Max, and much to be said.

"The mice in this churchyard must stop running free!

Let's hunt them all down! Let's have them for tea!

No mouse must escape us! No mice must be spared!

At sunrise tomorrow war will be declared!"

Ah the mice in the churchyard, they run free,
"I'll catch 'em!" snarled Holly. "You leave 'em to me!
My teeth are like razors, my claws are like knives!
I'll give those church mice the fright of their lives!"
He darkened his eyes, and he bared his sharp teeth,
Then he sprang from the bow of a funeral wreath.

"Snap!" went his sharp claws,
"Gotcha!" he hissed.
But when he opened his paws,
He found he had missed.

Ah the mice in the churchyard, they run free,
"Stand back," boasted Marble. "They won't escape me!
I'll nab 'em, I'll grab 'em, I'll show them who's boss.
I'll turn all their tails into cat dental floss!"
And he lowered his shoulders and prowled like a lion,
Past a tombstone railed with rusty old iron.

"I'm a mean ginger ninja, I catch mice for fun!"

And he crept and he leapt,

But his mouse count was none.

Ah the mice in the churchyard, they run free,
"Make way," purred a voice. "They haven't met me!
Millie's the name. I don't like to boast,
But my breakfast this morning will be church mice on toast."
And she slunk past the graves of some mouldering Kettles,
Crossed the church path and hid in the nettles.

With the poise and the pounce of a pedigree hero,

She flew from her hideout … but came back with zero.

Ah the mice in the churchyard, they run free,
"You're mincemeat!" growled Smokey. "You won't outrun me!"
And he leapt from a mound of freshly dug earth,
And chased round the fence for all he was worth.

Out through the brambles, in through the holly,

Twice round the headstone of old David Polley.

He scratched and he slashed and he yowled, and yet still …

The mice that he captured amounted to nil.

Ah the mice in the churchyard, they run free,
"Keep low!" whispered Harvey. "Surprise is the key!
I'll get 'em squealing, I'll make 'em squeak,
I've been planning my ambush for over a week!"
He sloped past the tomb of Elizabeth Fenn,
Said a quick prayer, and whispered amen.

Then he pounced on the mice with a screech and a wail,
But his claws captured nothing, not even a tail.

Ah the mice in the churchyard, they run free,
"Up here," hissed Spike from the top of a tree.
"If you want to catch mice you should climb up this yew,
from here you can take up an aerial view."
Spike winked from on high, then gave a low growl,
Parted the branches and dropped like an owl.

"Where did they go?" he screeched as he landed,
For the mice at his feet had somehow disbanded.

Ah the mice in the churchyard, they run free,
"No one gets the better of me!"
Striding across the grave of John Tampion,
Came Monty, the local mouse-catching champion.
With an arch of his back and a lick of his paws,
He polished his whiskers, then sharpened his claws.

He sashayed, he sauntered, he swaggered and swanked,

Singled three mice out – sprang, but then blanked.

Ah the mice in the churchyard, they run free,
Where four legs had failed, it was time to try three.
Bobby and Trio stepped into the ring,
Synchronised paws and got ready to spring.

"We know how to catch mice. We know all their tricks.
We may have three legs, but together we're six!"
And they flew at the grave of James Ambiolo,
But captured no more than the cats working solo.

Ah the mice in the churchyard, they run free,
"I think what we need is a group strategy."
Suki was right, if they all worked as one,
The mice in the churchyard would have nowhere to run.
The cats discussed tactics and formed a long line,
Then slowly moved in, one step at a time.
Tails raised like pike staffs, they advanced paw by paw,
But the mice turned and fled through the open church door!

Ah the mice in the churchyard, they run free,
Down the aisles, over pews, through the nave and vestry.
Round the font, over altar, through chancel and apse,
Up bell ropes and pulpit, through holes, cracks and gaps.
The cats charged in after them, a chorus of wails,
A whirlwind of whiskers, sharp teeth and tails.

They were mad, they were murderous, savage and seething,
You could heat a stone floor with the breath they were breathing.
"Let's nail 'em," yowled Elsa. "Let's squish 'em, let's squash 'em.
Let's capture the lot, share 'em out, and then nosh 'em!"

Fizzy gave chase in his marmalade stripes,
But the mice did a bunk down the organ pipes.

Pepper flew past in a blizzard of white,
But the mouse he was chasing jumped clean out of sight.

"I caught one!" yowled Hector. "I had one right here.
But it slipped through my claws and ran over my ear!"

"Me, too," miaowed Titus. "It was pinned to my chest,
But it jumped from my paws and ran off with the rest."
"Keep trying!" hissed Barney. "We can't let them win.
We must capture each one. We must do them all in!"

A frenzy of hissing and scrabbling claws,
Echoed the length of the gravestone-slabbed floors.
But the yowling and howling became huffing and puffing,
As all the cats caught was a churchload of nothing.

Ah the mice in the churchyard still run free,
"Go home," yawned the church cat. "Leave the mice be.
Despite all your howling and yowling and hissing,
All you've achieved, is a whole lot of missing.

Let the mice dance, let them play, let them roam.
Turn your tails round, and take yourself home.
You won't catch these mice, despite all your boasts,
For the mice in the churchyard are, all of them . . .

GHOSTS!"

Barney   Bobby   Bonny

Bono   Clyde   Daisy   Dillon✳   Edge   Elsa

Felix   Fizzy   Fred   Hamish McTavish   Harvey   Hector

Holly   Jazz   Jazz   Kitty   Maggie   Marble

Max   Mickey   Midnight   Miffy   Millie   Minnie

Minnow   Monty   Mr Bowlegs   Muffin   Pepper   Pink

Smartie   Smokey   Spike   Suki   Titus   Trio